# MY HEART– CHRIST'S HOME

## Retold for Children

................................................................

## ROBERT BOYD MUNGER

### with Carolyn Nystrom

*Illustrated by Jerry Tiritilli*

InterVarsity Press
Downers Grove, Illinois

Robert Boyd Munger:
  To Marilyn and Monica, who taught me how early
  and sensitively children respond to God's love.

Carolyn Nystrom:
  For David
  who learns with me

Jerry Tiritilli:
  For Christina Tiritilli

  Thanks also to those who served as artist's
  models for the illustrations: Joshua Lebak,
  Elizabeth Tiritilli, Cindy Lebak and Lena Reynolds.

©1997 by Robert Boyd Munger and Carolyn Nystrom

Illustrations ©1997 by Jerry Tiritilli

Cover illustration: Jerry Tiritilli

ISBN 0-8308-1907-X
Printed in the United States of America

Library of Congress Cataloging-in-Publication Data

Munger, Robert Boyd
    My heart—Christ's home retold for children/Robert Boyd Munger
with Carolyn Nystrom: illustrations by Jerry Tiritilli.
        p.    cm.
    Summary: In this story based on the author's sermon, a young boy
learns what it means to accept Jesus into his life.
    ISBN 0-8308-1907-X (alk. paper)
    1. Jesus Christ—Juvenile fiction. [Jesus Christ—Fiction.]
2. Christian life—Fiction.]   I. Nystrom, Carolyn.  II. Tiritilli,
Jerry, ill.  III. Title.
PZ7.M9236My  1997
[E]—dc21                                              97-12919
                                                        CIP
                                                        AC

15   14   13   12   11   10   9   8   7   6   5   4   3   2   1
05   04   03   02   01   00   99   98   97

Jesus came to my house. He walked up the steps and knocked softly at the door.

I peeked out. "It's Jesus!" I shouted. "Come into my house. We will have wonderful fun together."

I opened the door and Jesus stepped in. "Hello, Peter," he said. His smile was as warm as sunshine, his hug as big as the summer sky.

I led Jesus to our back porch. Mom was making lunch there—
juicy peaches and
crispy celery and
mushy peanut butter with currant jelly.
Mom looked up and smiled. "Please eat lunch with us," she said.
Jesus prayed, "Thank you, Father, for our food."
"Amen," we all said. Then we ate.

I like your willow tree," Jesus said. "I remember when my Father and I thought up willow trees. We wanted branches that dance with the wind, then bow low to kiss the ground."

"Sometimes I dance with the wind in the branches," I said. I jumped up and danced with the branches all around. Jesus danced too.

"I knew you would like that tree, Peter," Jesus said.

$L$et me show you our house," I said. I took Jesus' hand and led him inside.

"This is our kitchen," I said.

Jesus looked all around. "Did you help your mom make lunch here?" he asked.

I was glad that today I could say yes.

Then I led Jesus to a doorway down the hall. "This is my room," I said. "I sleep here. I do my homework at this desk. I play with my trucks and make puzzles on this rug. Sometimes my friends sleep over on that bed."

Jesus put his arm on my shoulder and looked all around my room. "I like your room," he said. "It looks like you."

Just then I noticed a small wooden box peeking out from under the bed. I tapped it with my heel and pushed it further underneath. I hoped Jesus didn't see it.

This is our living room," I said next.

My sister Janet was watching TV. She smiled and patted the seat next to her. I sat down, but Jesus kept standing in the doorway. On TV, I saw one man shoot another. I looked at Jesus. His eyes were sad. So I got up and headed outdoors. Jesus followed. Janet didn't seem to see Jesus at all. I wondered why.

Jesus and I played all day. I showed him my favorite place by the stream. We held tadpoles in our hands. A huge frog boomed, "CROOOAK!" We laughed.

"Oh, Peter," Jesus said, "I'm glad I made frogs."

That evening, Mom invited Jesus to spend the night. "You can stay in my room," I said. "I'll help get your bed ready."

We climbed into bed. Mom left the door ajar so I could see the light in the hall. I tried not to look too hard at all the shadows in the room.

"Peter, are you afraid?" Jesus asked.

"N-n-n—," I started to say. But I could feel Jesus looking straight at me through the dark. "Yes," I whispered. "I'm afraid a lot."

We talked a long time. We talked about

scary dreams and

monsters and

fingers tapping at my window and

big guys on the playground and

making mistakes that make people laugh at me.

With Jesus in the bed next to mine, none of that seemed very scary. I don't remember closing my eyes. I must have fallen asleep while Jesus was talking.

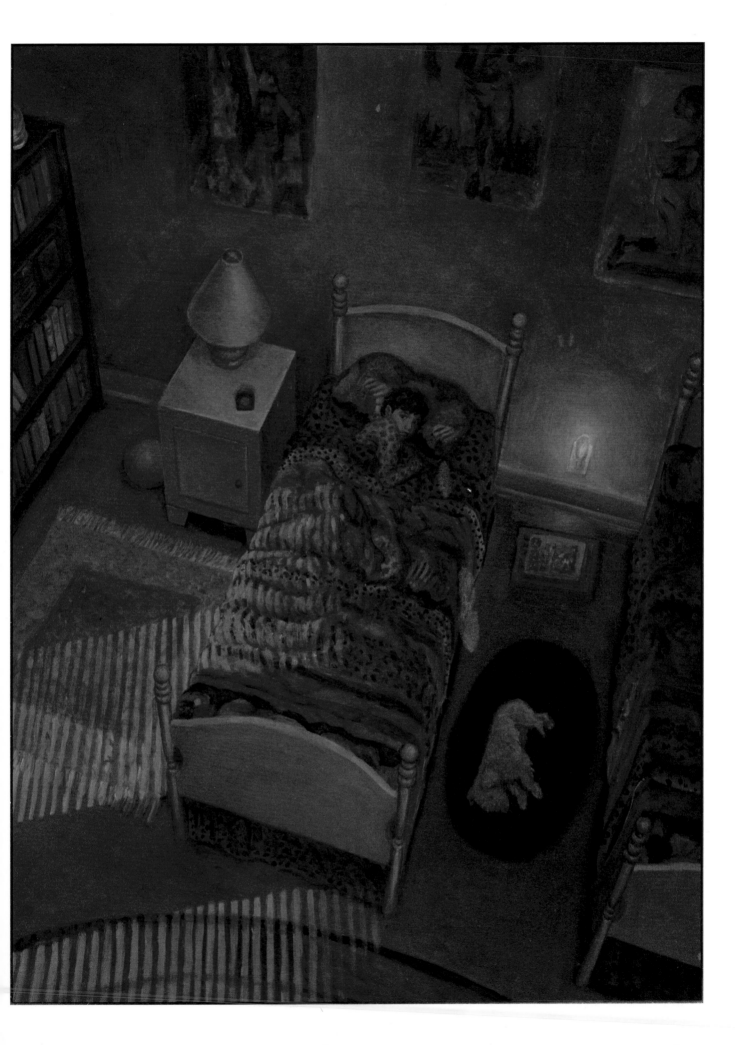

In the morning Jesus waited by the door to walk to school with me. Nobody noticed Jesus sitting beside me at my desk. I liked having him there.

The teacher began to explain our work. She wrote on the overhead while she talked. I tried to keep up, but I couldn't watch and write and listen at the same time. I got scared and mad too. Maybe I'd get everything wrong. Maybe she would ask me a question. Maybe I would say something dumb and everyone would laugh.

I wished she would slow down, but she went faster and faster. I wanted to cry. "Help me, Jesus," I whispered.

Jesus put his hand over mine. "Just listen, now," he whispered back. "Listen and think. You can write later."

I felt more calm. I didn't get everything right, but I got most of it. "Thank you, Jesus," I said.

After school my friends and I played soccer. Jesus walked up and down the sidelines, like a coach.

I am good at soccer, and I play to win. I was the goalie, so the ball kept coming at me and at me and at me. I stopped it with my hands, knees, feet. I even got a header.

Suddenly the ball came at me again—fast. There must have been eight guys behind it. I slammed my whole body down on the ball. But the ball was just inside the goal. I scrunched myself a little to the outside. The ball came too. Then I jumped up.

"It's out," I yelled.

"Is not," the other team yelled back. "You moved it!"

My best buddy, Jake, was on the other team. He was yelling just as hard as anyone.

"Cheat!" he screamed right into my face.

Then everything got quiet. Nobody wanted to play anymore. I didn't either.

I walked home hot and tired and dirty. I didn't say much to Jesus on the way.

At home, I found my darkest pencil. I wrote something on a small piece of paper. I burrowed under my bed and dug out my box. I lifted the lid and looked inside. Yes, it was all still there. I threw in the paper and snapped the lid shut. Then I kicked the box back under my bed.

I saw Mom and Jesus in the kitchen. They were talking quietly at the table. I didn't feel like being with them, so I started toward the TV. I heard Mom say to Jesus, "I'm so glad you are here. Will you live with us always?"

Mom didn't even ask me first! I liked having Jesus visit my house, but living with us was something else. It felt funny having Jesus watch *everything* I did.

"I will be glad to make my home with you," I heard Jesus answer.

I edged out of the kitchen and went back to my room. I dug my box out from under my bed. I buried it in the darkest corner of my closet. Then I closed the door tight.

That night Jesus slept on the bed in my room again. We didn't talk much. I noticed that he didn't sleep very well. Neither did I.

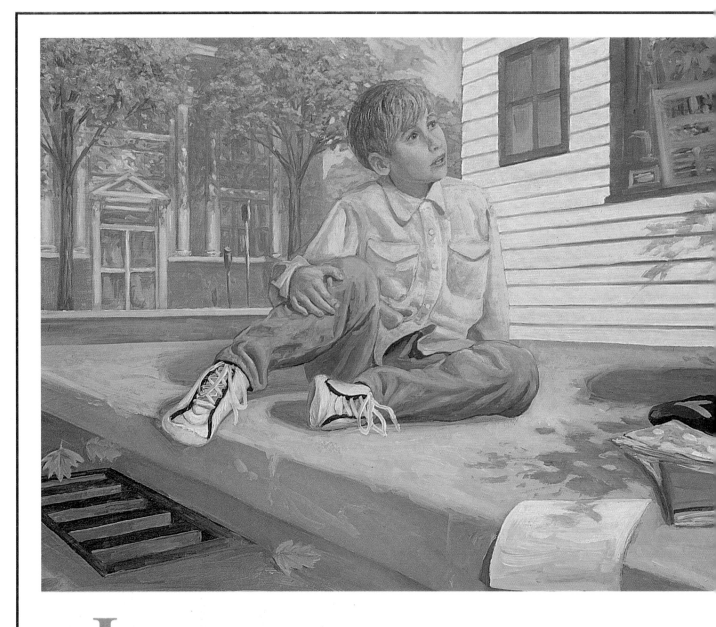

I got up early and ducked out the door fast. I wanted to walk to school by myself. As I crossed the schoolyard, I thought I saw a shadow next to me. It didn't look like mine. When I looked again, the shadow was gone.

I didn't see Jesus all day at school, but I saw that funny shadow once in a while. Math class was hard. We are learning to multiply. Everyone seemed to get it but me. I wished I could ask Jesus for help.

At recess Jake said, "Hi." I acted like I didn't hear him.

After school I pretended I was a football player carrying the ball. I put my head down and ran for home.

Suddenly I felt a strong arm shove against my chest. I sat down hard on the sidewalk. A truck thundered past just inches from my shoes.

"Jesus," I gasped. "Have you been with me all day?"

"Yes," he said.

"But I didn't see you."

"Did you want to see me, Peter?" he asked quietly.

"No," I answered. I felt embarrassed, but I had to tell him the truth.

"I knew you wanted to be alone," he said.

"Thanks for keeping me safe," I whispered.

That night I climbed into bed and pulled up the covers. But Jesus sat on the edge of his bed.

"I don't think I can stay in this room tonight," he said. "It smelled so awful last night that I couldn't sleep. I think it's coming from the closet."

"Maybe it's my sneakers," I said.

"It's not sneakers," Jesus said. "I don't mind the smell of sneakers at all." He rolled up the bedding. "I'll sleep on the porch tonight," he said as he walked out.

I stayed awake a long time. There *was* a funny smell coming from my closet. I knew what it was. It was hidden in the farthest corner, and it was mine.

My room seemed extra dark. The shadows seemed extra large. I knew the tapping at my window was just a branch on the bush outside. But it scared me anyway.

I missed Jesus.

In the morning I ran to the porch. Jesus sat up and stretched. "I dreamed I was dancing with the willow tree," he said. "When I woke up, the willow was tickling my beard."

We both laughed.

We ate breakfast on the porch. I like Saturday.

After breakfast Jesus said, "Well, my friend, we have work to do. It's time to tackle your closet."

"But it's *my* closet." I tried not to yell. "Those are *my* things. I like them just the way they are."

"If you want me to live with you," Jesus said, "we will have to get rid of that stink."

We walked down the hall together. I could smell something awful even before we got to the door.

I crawled into the darkest, farthest corner of the closet. Slowly I put my hands on my wooden box. Slowly I brought it out.

Together we pried open the lid. I wished no one had to see what was inside:

Two shiny wings I pulled off a live butterfly.

A small car I took from Jake's house last summer.

A scribbled note in dark angry letters. *I hate you, Jake,* it said.

Jesus looked a long time at all the things in my box. His face was sad. But in a funny way, he looked like he loved me.

"I'm sorry," I said.

"I forgive you," Jesus answered. And he held me with a huge hug.

"Do you want me to stay with you always?" Jesus asked.

"Yes," I answered. This time I was sure.

"We will give the car back to Jake," Jesus said. "But you must let me keep the box."

"That's all right," I said. "I don't want it anymore."

When I am with you, other people may not see me," Jesus told me.

"I know."

"Here is the hard part," Jesus said. "You may not always see me either—even when you want to."

"I want you with me anyway. I belong to you."

"Then I will make my home with you." Jesus smiled.

"Even when I am afraid?"

"Especially when you are afraid," Jesus said. "I will live with you forever," he added.

"Forever," I echoed.

# NOTE TO THE PARENT

What happens when Jesus enters our lives? I hope that this adaptation of Robert Boyd Munger's powerful sermon will provide an opportunity for you to talk with your child about what it means to give our lives to Jesus.

First, just enjoy the story. Of course it is layered with meaning, but for the first several readings just have fun with it. Some of those meanings will soak in even without full explanation.

Then begin to talk about Jesus as this story reveals him. Your child may notice that Jesus made frogs and willow trees (Jesus was present at creation). Jesus hugs Peter and plays with him (Jesus loves us). Jesus felt sad about the violence on TV (Jesus hates sin). Jesus helped Peter at school (Jesus helps us through hard times). Jesus saved Peter from the truck (Jesus can protect us). Jesus went to school with Peter even when Peter didn't want him there (Jesus stays with us no matter what). Some people could not see Jesus (not everyone believes in Jesus). Jesus told Peter to get rid of the box of sins (Jesus expects his people to be holy). Jesus helped Peter open the box (Jesus will help us to stop doing what is wrong). Jesus took the box and forgave Peter (Jesus erases our sins and forgives us). Jesus will live with Peter forever (Jesus is making an eternal home for us in heaven).

But will a real, live, visible Jesus come and knock at our door someday? Most children will see that this part of the story is imagination—just as Munger's story imagined that Jesus lived in his house. But it is an imagination that helps us see how real and how personal is the relationship that Jesus invites. May this retelling of Munger's story encourage you and your child in your walk with him.

*Carolyn Nystrom*

## *The Story of* MY HEART—CHRIST'S HOME

The sermon "My Heart—Christ's Home" was first preached in the fall of 1947 early in my pastorate at the First Presbyterian Church of Berkeley. It was an evening service. The congregation was composed largely of young people, students and a sprinkling of stalwart older saints. I loved these informal hours of fellowship. I was able to share Christ more personally and fully than in the worship services of the morning. The evening sermon was not written out in manuscript form but simply outlined and preached from notes.

I remember the occasion distinctly. Shortly after beginning the sermon I was surprised to see Dr. Henrietta Mears of the Hollywood Presbyterian Church slip quietly into a back pew. Henrietta was a very dear friend of both my wife, Edith, and mine. She had influenced our lives for Christ profoundly as she had so many hundreds of other young men and women. In fact, our wedding reception had been in her home. Her unexpected visit, however, stirred a conflict of feelings. I was delighted to have her with us but dismayed that she was not the one doing the preaching. Why had she not come to the morning service when I was better prepared?

Her comment at the conclusion of the service put my mind at rest. "You must give that message at the Forest Home Briefing Conference this summer!"

With this encouragement from Henrietta and a few others in attendance that evening, I ventured to share the outline of the sermon the following February with an InterVarsity Christian Fellowship group near Chicago while participating in a series of chapel services at Wheaton College. Someone recorded the message on a wire recorder, the antecedent of the modern tape recorder. A student transcribed a rough copy of the talk and mimeographed it to circulate among a few friends.

In due course a copy came into the hands of an editor at InterVarsity Press. In 1948 I received a letter asking permission—which I granted—to print the sermon for wider distribution as a booklet. No contract was signed as neither of us anticipated it would be widely read. Not until six years later was it edited for inclusion in a book of my sermons, *What Jesus Said* (Revell, 1954).

I have been told that about ten million copies of the booklet *My Heart—Christ's Home* have been distributed in over a dozen languages throughout the world. In 1986 I updated and expanded the InterVarsity Press booklet a bit. In 1992 a gift book edition was produced by InterVarsity Press, and I was able to further expand the material. Then, in 1994 InterVarsity Press released a Bible study guide to accompany my booklet.

This children's edition follows the original idea of portraying the believer as a host to the indwelling Christ in the home of the heart. Rather than moving from room to room in the house of the heart and looking at different aspects of discipleship, this edition emphasizes the relationship we build with Jesus when we invite him to join us in all of life.

Daily I need to make sure that the title deeds of ownership of my life are held firmly in Jesus' hands—that my heart might truly be his home. May Christ be with you and your children as you also make a place for him in your home.

*Robert Boyd Munger*